THIS CANDLEWICK BOOK BELONGS TO:

_____

_____

_____

_____

This book is dedicated to the memory of Ben,
a boy who loved animals

Copyright © 1990 by Sarah Hayes

All rights reserved.

First U.S. paperback edition 1996

Library of Congress Cataloging-in-Publication Data

Hayes, Sarah.

Nine ducks nine / Sarah Hayes. —1st U.S. paperback ed.

Summary: As Mr. Fox watches and draws closer
to nine ducks, one by one they drop out of sight.

ISBN 1-56402-830-5

[1. Ducks—Fiction.  2. Foxes—Fiction.  3. Counting.]  I. Title.

PZ7.H314873Ni     1996

[E]—dc20           95-38453

2 4 6 8 10 9 7 5 3  .

Printed in Hong Kong

This book was typeset in ITC Garamond.
The pictures were done in watercolor and ink.

Candlewick Press
2067 Massachusetts Avenue
Cambridge, Massachusetts 02140

# Nine Ducks Nine

Sarah Hayes

**CANDLEWICK PRESS**
CAMBRIDGE, MASSACHUSETTS

Nine ducks nine walked out in line.

Mr. Fox was watching.

One duck ran away,

down to the rickety bridge.

We'll get that fox

Eight ducks eight sat on the gate.

Mr. Fox came through the woods.

One duck ran away,

down to the rickety bridge.

Seven ducks seven took off together.

Mr. Fox came out of the woods.

One duck flew away,

down to the rickety bridge.

Six ducks six did balancing tricks.

Mr. Fox came closer.

One duck ran away,

down to the rickety bridge.

Five ducks five began to dive.

Mr. Fox came closer.

One duck swam away,

down to the rickety bridge.

Four ducks four reached the shore.

Mr. Fox came closer and closer.

One duck flew away,

down to the rickety bridge.

Three ducks three flew into a tree.

Mr. Fox came closer and closer.

One duck flew away,

down to the rickety bridge.

Two ducks two had things to do.

Mr. Fox came even closer.

One duck crept away,

to the end of the rickety bridge.

One duck one sat in the sun,
all alone on the rickety bridge.

Mr. Fox came right up close and . . .

# Mr. Fox pounced!

The rickety bridge broke and
# SPLASH!
Mr. Fox fell into the river.

Nine ducks nine swam back in line.
Mr. Fox went home to his den
and never chased those ducks again.

SARAH HAYES says the story for *Nine Ducks Nine* comes first from her love of folk stories in which the wily fox is outwitted. She was inspired to write about ducks because of the duck pond near her home. "The ducks always cross the road in a long line of big white ducks followed by a little brown duck at the end." She adds, "Children count forward easily, but often find counting backward very difficult. I wanted to write a story that would make subtraction fun." Sarah Hayes is also the author-illustrator of *The Cats of Tiffany Street* and the author of *This Is the Bear, This Is the Bear and the Bad Little Girl*, and *The Candlewick Book of Fairy Tales*.